This book was made especially for:

JULIETTE

Dear Juliette,

Words cannot express how special you are.
But, here are twenty-six that try! Each one so
perfectly describes you. You are all of these
wonderful qualities— and so much more.

Love,

A is for *amazing.*
That's Juliette
in every way!

B

is for the special way you *brighten* up each day.

C
is for your *courage*. You don't fear what to do.

D

is for your *daring.*
You always
carry through.

E is for your *energy*, so vibrant and so bright!

F

is for the *fun*
you bring to all
both day and night.

G describes your future.
Oh, the places
you will *go!*

H is for the *heights* you'll climb and successes you will know.

I's *imagination* and the power of your dreams.

J

is for the *joy* you bring, your shining face that beams.

K is for your *kindness*,
shown to big and small.

L

is for the *love*
you freely share
with one and all.

M
is for your *music*,
the song of your
own heart.

N is meant for *never*,
for we'll never,
ever part.

O means there is *one* you—there never will be two!

P is meant for *perfect*—it's you just being you.

Q is all the *qualities*
I notice every time.

R is how you're *rare*, like a diamond from a mine.

S is meant for *super*, for you have pow'r to soar!

T is for the *talents* that you have (and so much more!)

U
is for *unique* in every bold sense of the word.

V is for your *voice.* Don't be afraid that you'll be heard!

W

is for *wild.*
Always live and
gallop free!

X

is xceptional,
xtraordinarily!

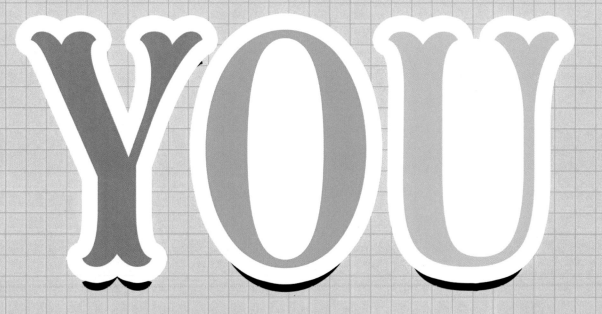

YOU

Y is meant for *you*, the only one there'll ever be.

But day is done, and you must sleep, so

Z now stands for zzzzzzzzzzz...

Li'l Llama

CUSTOM KIDS BOOKS

Cover and book design by David Miles

Made in the USA
Las Vegas, NV
12 December 2024